PARACHUTE BRANCH LIBRARY
Phone: 970-285-9870
244 Grand Valley Way
Parachute, CO 81635

D1370312

Brave Martha

*For Sophie, Elaine,
and Walter Lorraine*

The text of this book is set in 20-point Goudy.
The illustrations are pencil with watercolor on paper.

Library of Congress Cataloging-in-Publication Data

Apple, Margot.
Brave Martha / written and illustrated by Margot Apple.
p. cm.
Summary: One night when she has to go to bed without her cat Sophie,
Martha worries about all the things she sees and hears in the dark.
ISBN 0-395-59422-7
[1. Cats — Fiction. 2. Fear of the dark — Fiction.
3. Bedtime — Fiction.] I. Title.
PZ7.A6474BR   1999
[E] — dc21   97-42616 CIP AC

Manufactured in the United States of America
WOZ 10 9 8 7 6 5 4 3 2

Brave Martha

written and illustrated

by Margot Apple

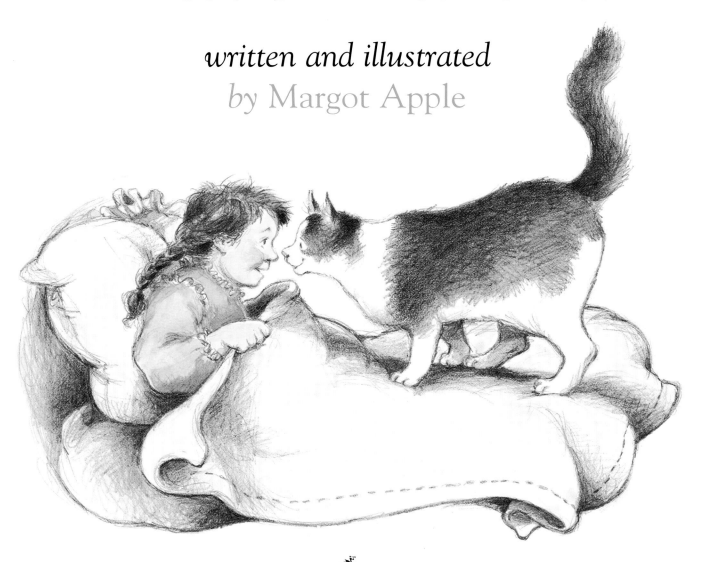

Houghton Mifflin Company   Boston

Once there was a little girl.
Her name was Martha.
She lived in a big old house
with her mother and her father
and Sophie.

Every morning,
Martha gave Sophie
crunchies and milk.
Martha patted her,
and Sophie purred.

In the afternoon,
Martha and Sophie
went walking.
Sometimes they would
dress up.

And every night, Sophie helped Martha get ready for bed. Martha brushed her teeth. Sophie watched the water go down the drain.

Then they walked all
the way down the hall.
Sophie always went first.

At the bedroom door
Martha waited
while Sophie checked
all the creepy places.

When Sophie came out from under the bed Martha knew it was safe.

One night Martha's parents had company. The guests brought their dog.

When bedtime came, Martha couldn't find Sophie anywhere. So Father had to help her get ready for bed.

Father glanced around the bedroom. Then he said,
"Oh, be brave, Martha. There's nothing under the bed.
Now hop in and I'll read you a story."

When he finished reading, Father kissed Martha good night.
Then he took his little flashlight out of his pocket and put
it in her hand. "Just in case you need it," he said.

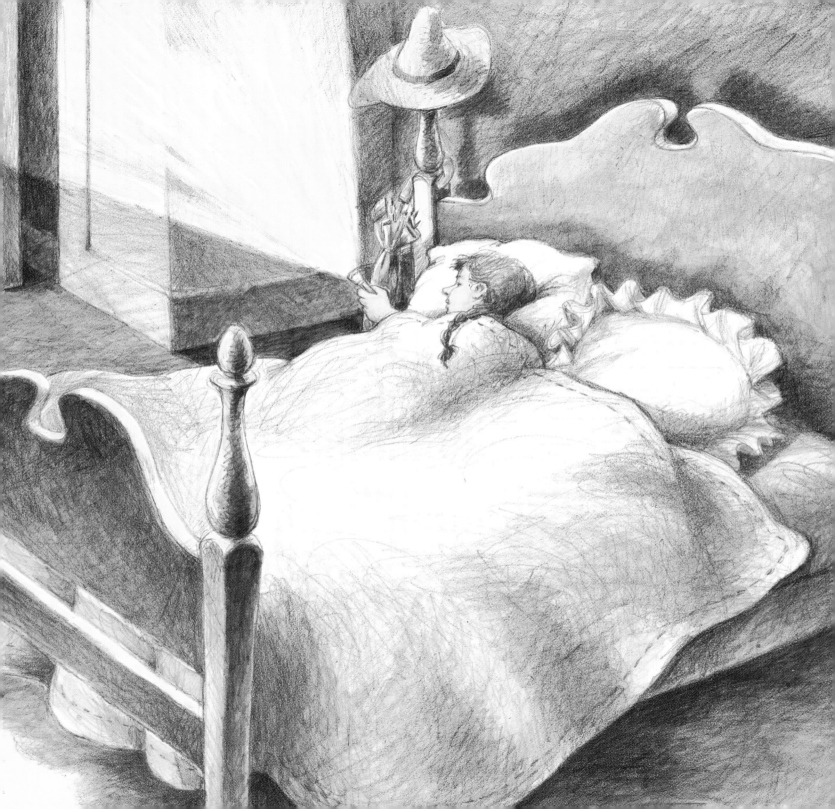

The clock ticked. The guests talked.
Finally they said good night.
The front door closed.
Mother and Father turned out the
lights and came upstairs.
The house was absolutely still.
That's when Martha heard it.
Scritcha, scritcha, scritch.

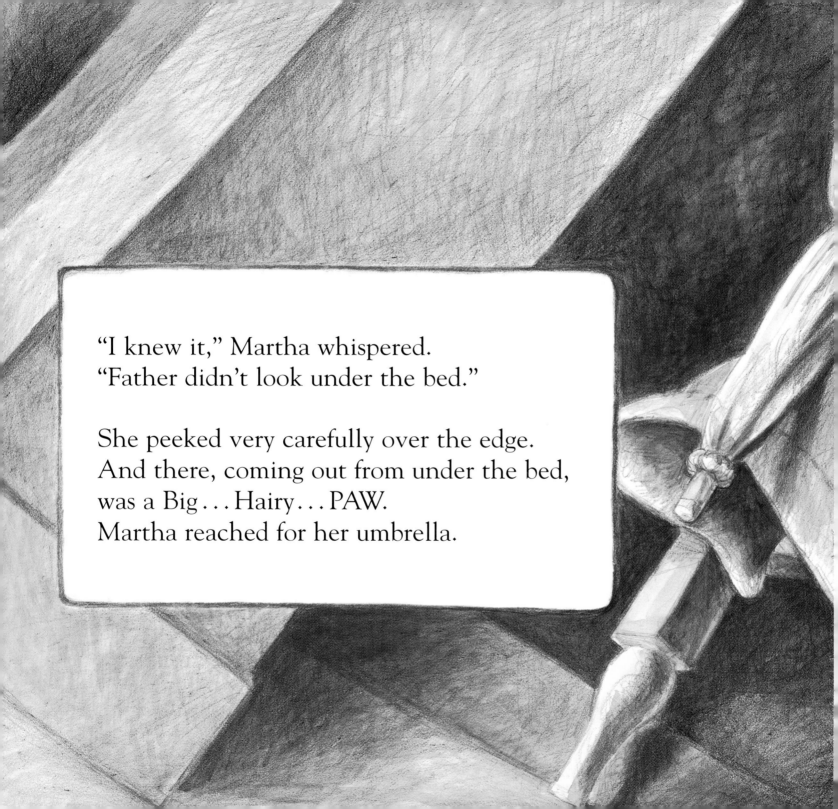

"I knew it," Martha whispered.
"Father didn't look under the bed."

She peeked very carefully over the edge.
And there, coming out from under the bed,
was a Big...Hairy...PAW.
Martha reached for her umbrella.

"CHA!" Martha jumped.
KLONK went the umbrella.
"My Daniel Boone hat," she croaked.
Martha felt all shaky, like Jell-o.
She put the hat on. It was warm and soft.

Martha was about to climb back in bed
when . . . *Scritcha, scritcha, scritch!*
There it was again.

Martha peeked at the closet.
"It's in there. Oh dear, it's got horns . . .
but wait, Martha," she whispered.
"Monsters hate light. It makes them weak.
Where's that flashlight?"

"HAH," cried Martha, grabbing the flashlight.
"When the light hits it, it'll faint!"
She poked the door open.
She aimed the light into the closet.

"Owl?" Martha blurted.
"I forgot you were in there."
She swooped him up and
flopped down on the bed.

Scritcha, scritcha, scritch, scraaaape!
There it was again, louder than
ever! It was coming from the dresser.
The middle drawer wiggled.
Slowly it opened inch by inch.
All at once there were two big yellow
eyes staring back at Martha.
She screamed, "EEEK!"

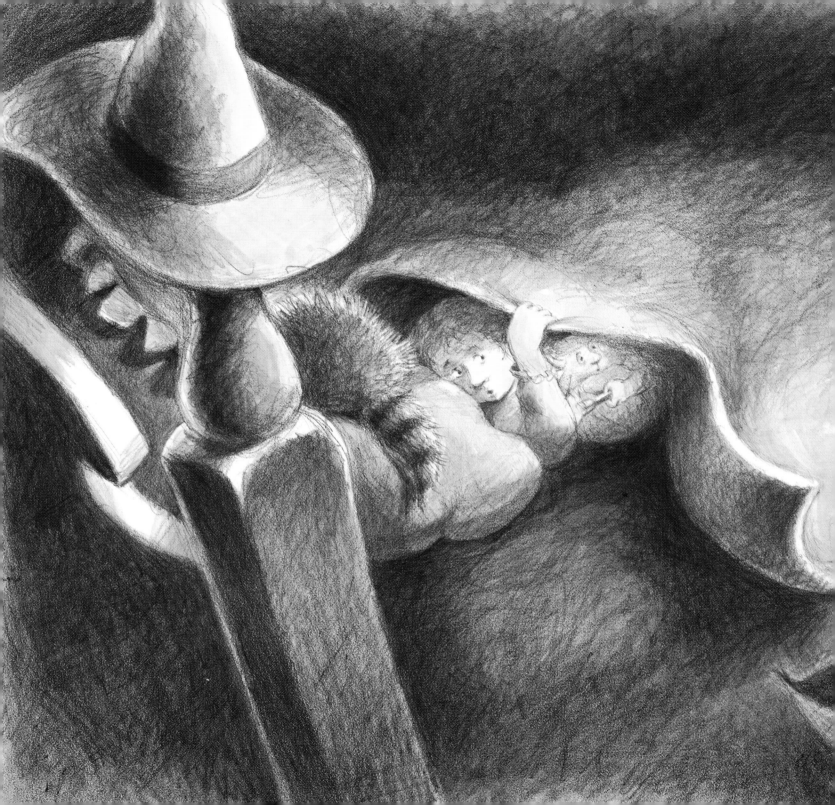

"Papa," Martha cried. Then she heard a shuffle and a grunt followed by a tremendous THUD. There was a *thump, thump, thump* coming toward the bed.

"Oof!" said Martha. Something landed on her. It was so heavy that she couldn't breathe.

"Help!" she gasped.

It answered, "Prrrt purrrt purr."
"Oh, Sophie, it's you!"
Martha hugged Sophie tight.
"Now we can go to sleep."
And they did.